AF271283

We would like to dedicate this book to Julie Hildebrand, a young cancer survivor who inspired us to follow our dream to finally write a children's book.

www.mascotbooks.com

Iggy's Second Chance

For more information, please contact:
Mascot Kids, an imprint of Amplify Publishing Group
620 Herndon Parkway, Suite 320
Herndon, VA 20170
info@mascotbooks.com

Library of Congress Control Number: 2022945165

CPSIA Code: PRKF1022A

ISBN-13: 978-1-63755-060-1

Printed in China

Iggy's Second Chance
Patricia Paradiso & Laura DeAngelis
Illustrated by Jeffrey Mora

Hi! My name is Iggy, and I live in Louisiana with the Landry family. Easton and Evelyn are the parents of Elijah and Emma, and we all live together! Every day, I keep Elijah company while he trains for high school track. I help Emma with her homework. When Easton cooks barbecue, he always gives me a tasty snack after Emma finishes an assignment. Life is good. I love my family. We don't always have the most money, but they always keep my food bowl full!

While life has always been pretty sunny, I'm beginning to get worried. Lately, my family keeps talking about hurricanes. It gets very hot and humid in the summer, and the sky gets very dark and scary. Papa Easton has been frowning a lot, so I know he is concerned. When I hear him telling the family that they have to go to a local shelter because a hurricane is coming right through our town, I can tell that everything is going to change.

"I don't like to swim! Could the house flood?" Emma asks. "But what do we do with Iggy?"

Papa says, "We will leave Iggy upstairs and come back for him in a day or two. They don't allow dogs in shelters."

I am so scared, but I know my family will come back for me. After all, it's only a day or two.

The next day, Emma kisses me goodbye
and leaves me plenty of food and water.

She tells me to stay on her bed and curl up in a blanket if I start to get cold.
I can see tears in her eyes, and I know this is not going to be good.

I can tell when the hurricane hits the house when a very loud thundering hurts my ears and the heavy rain and wind shakes the walls. I usually cuddle with Emma during storms, so until then I go under her bed.

When all the noise finally dies down, I jump out
of the bedroom window. I am nervous and run as
fast as I can. Maybe I can find my family!

After wandering the wet streets, I come upon another dog.
After giving each other a good sniff, I find out her name is Rocky.
She's looking for her family too, so we will help each other sniff
together! Rocky barks a lot, but she's a good friend. She's a tough pup
with a lot of confidence. I am glad I found her. I convince Rocky to come
back to my house. Surely the Landrys would take her in, too!

But as I approach my block, my usual walk route looked very different. There was no house anymore. Just debris. I begin to cry. Rocky accompanies me as I sniff around to find anything from my old life.

The only thing left is my favorite bone. It smells like Emma's bed. Thank goodness I have Rocky here for me now.

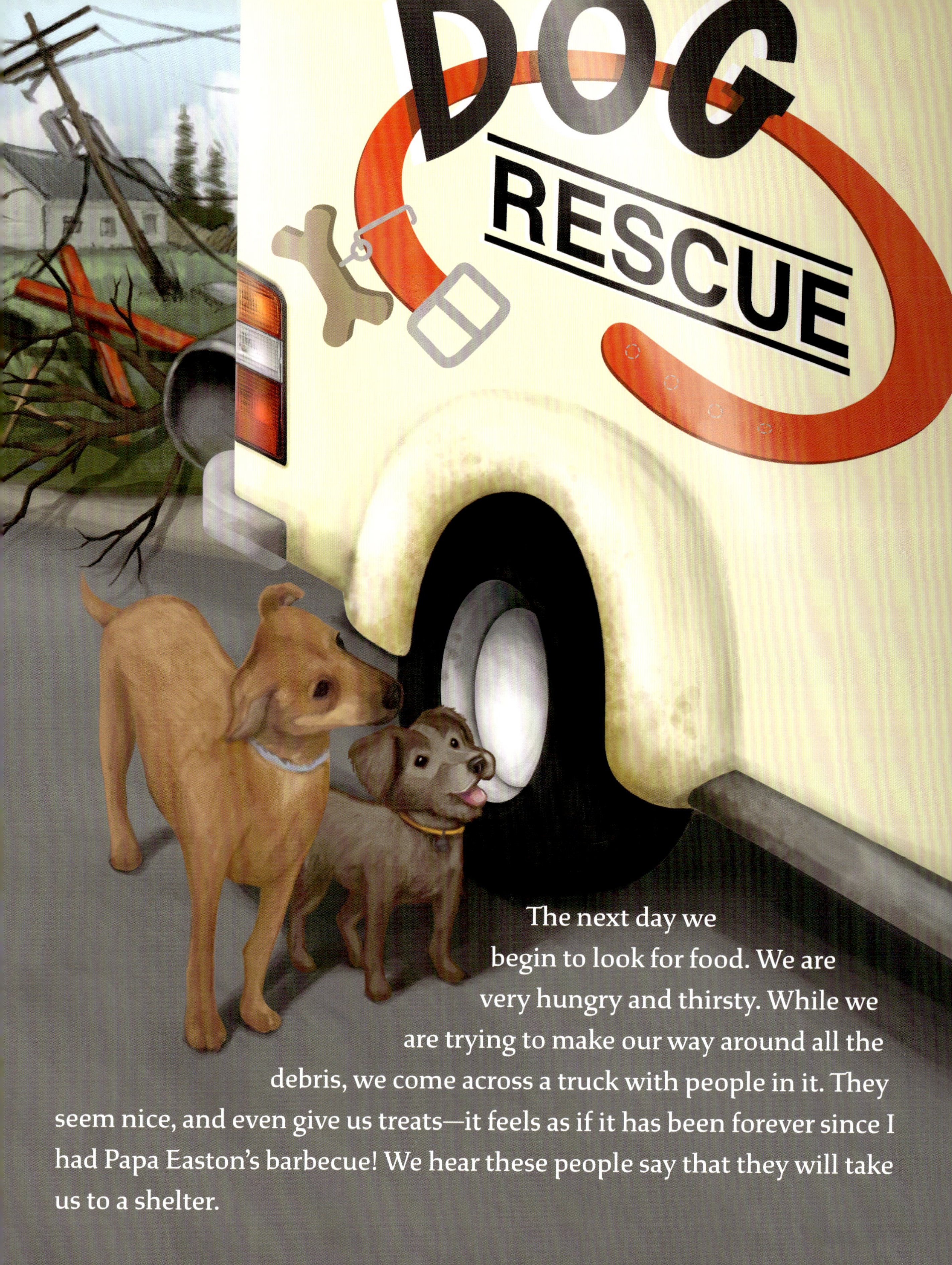

The next day we begin to look for food. We are very hungry and thirsty. While we are trying to make our way around all the debris, we come across a truck with people in it. They seem nice, and even give us treats—it feels as if it has been forever since I had Papa Easton's barbecue! We hear these people say that they will take us to a shelter.

"Maybe we will even get adopted together," she says.

But I don't want another family. I want to be with the Landrys.

We are taken to a hospital where they give us medicine and lots of shots. They also put a computer chip in each of our necks. The shots hurt, and all of this is so new, but Rocky assures me we will see our families again. The shelter takes good care of us, but after a few days, we still aren't back together with our families. I am so sad that I don't even want to eat.

Eventually, we are loaded onto a big truck in separate cages with many other animals. The humans tell us we will be transported to a shelter in New Jersey so we can be adopted by new families. Why were they taking me away from my home? I am so sad, but my pal Rocky keeps telling me to have faith.

It is a very long, bumpy ride to New Jersey, but eventually we
arrive at an animal welfare center. Rocky is right alongside me the whole
time. Throughout the journey, Rocky tells me to just keep thinking happy
thoughts, because a new family will come along and give us a great home.
She says, "Sometimes you have to go through some hard times to
get to a better place." Rocky seems like a very wise
dog. She's definitely my "rock."

WELCOME
TO
NEW JERSEY
THE GARDEN STATE

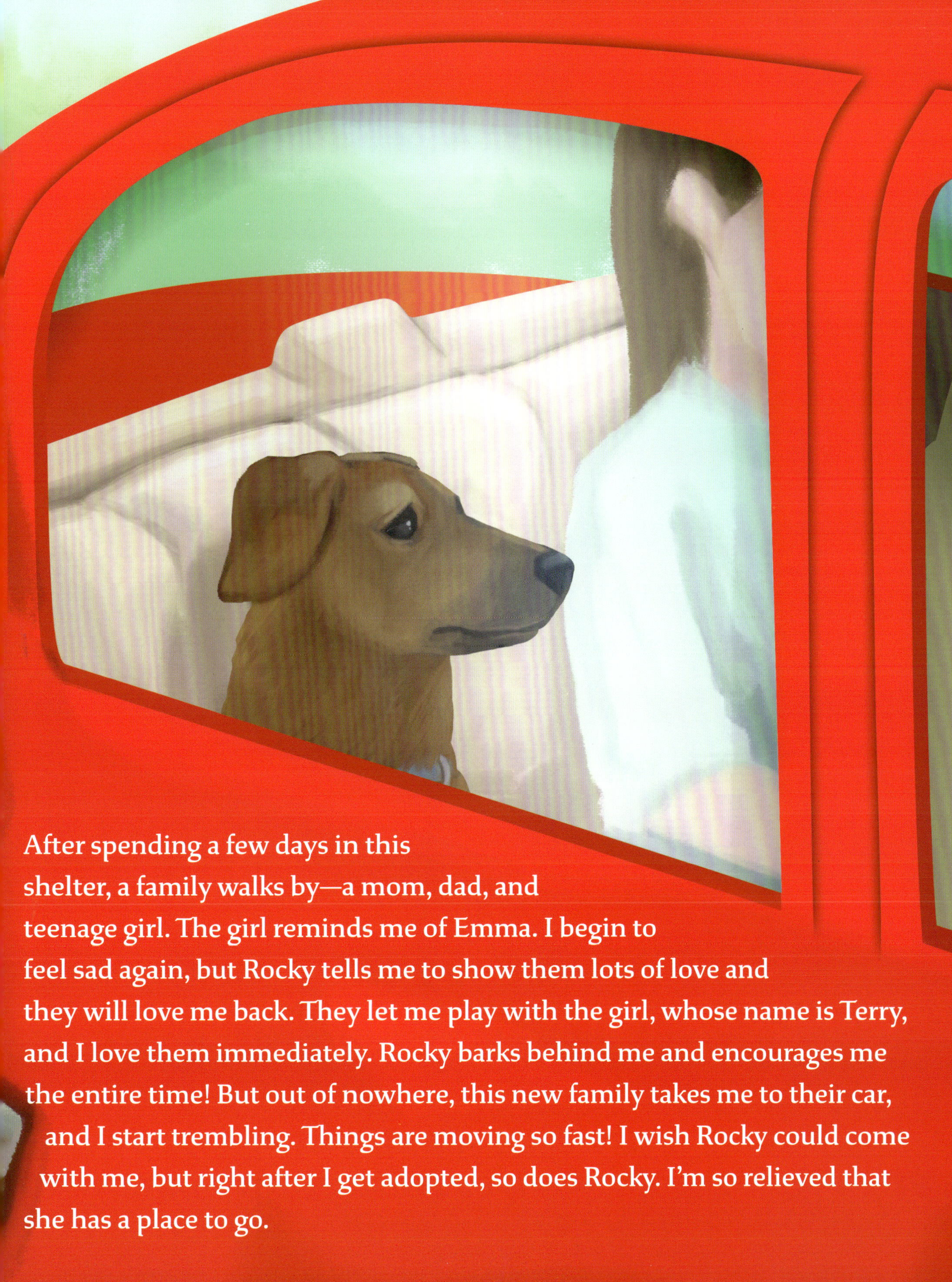

After spending a few days in this
shelter, a family walks by—a mom, dad, and
teenage girl. The girl reminds me of Emma. I begin to
feel sad again, but Rocky tells me to show them lots of love and
they will love me back. They let me play with the girl, whose name is Terry,
and I love them immediately. Rocky barks behind me and encourages me
the entire time! But out of nowhere, this new family takes me to their car,
and I start trembling. Things are moving so fast! I wish Rocky could come
with me, but right after I get adopted, so does Rocky. I'm so relieved that
she has a place to go.

This new family gives me lots of hugs and kisses, and they feed me very well. Terry even lets me sleep on her bed! My new dad takes me on long walks, and I am making lots of new friends. They even have a guinea pig named Emil. One day we will play together, but, for now, it's sniffs only! I hear Rocky's new family is also loving, and we may even get a playdate together!

I miss the Landrys very much, and I am sure they miss me too. I think of Emma every time Terry does her homework, and I think of Papa Easton when my dad cooks me a special meal. Maybe one day I will see them again, but until then, they will always be with me in my heart. I hear that they will be able to rebuild their house, but for now, they are safe and living with relatives.

Rocky was right. When you think positively and have faith, it can definitely make a bad situation better. And having the support of a good friend like Rocky gave me the strength to keep looking up.

Change is scary, but I am so happy to have gotten a great
second chance.

"My family went to a shelter!" I tell Rocky. We are saved!

FOOD

About the Author

Patricia Paradiso has been a pediatric nurse for over thirty-five years, and always wanted to write a children's book to help children cope with illnesses. She adopted her dog, Iggy, two years ago and observed firsthand what rescue animals endure. She wants children to understand the hardships of rescues and learn the value of developing friendships when confronted with adversity. Her daughter and co-author, Laura, also adopted a rescue named Elaine, who has been a great support to her. Patricia is hoping *Iggy's Second Chance* will encourage adoption or volunteering at rescues. Patricia's other hobbies include cycling, long walks, reading, and volunteering at local rescues.

About the Author

Laura DeAngelis and her rescue chihuahua, Elaine, moved together from Chicago, to New Jersey, and then all the way to Berlin. As an artist, Laura lives a very fast-paced lifestyle, and Elaine is right there with her through all of it. With all of this change and movement, one thing that is consistent for Laura and Elaine is their bond to each other. Laura and Patricia hope this book will show you that there is reality behind the cliche "who rescued who?" Without Laura, Elaine might still be in a shelter in Oklahoma. Without Elaine, Laura may lack the consistent love and grounding a dog provides during all of life's challenges. Laura's other interests include yoga, dance, and photography.